The Ipswich Bus

The Ipswich Bus

by

Robbie

The Ipswich Bus

A collection of extraordinary poems for ordinary people, written by Robbie, a fairly ordinary but talented man. If you like your poetry complicated, then this is not the book for you. Robbie writes in a way that is both heart-warming and relatable.
But be prepared for both laughter and tears along the way.

All or any proceeds from the sale of this book will be donated directly to "The Ipswich Outreach Bus Project", which is a small charity aiming to raise money to buy and convert a bus which will be utilised to help the homeless and those in need.

http://www.ipswichoutreachbus.co.uk/

I hope you enjoy the read as much as I did.

Mandy Rigby

****

A Cuddle

You once told me how a cuddle
Was like an act of faith
And to have my arms around you
You somehow felt more safe
That most basic of enclosures
Was the greatest of them all
And would always mean much more to you
Than the poshest set of walls.

Adrift

I'm drifting round our Mother Earth
And view this wondrous scene
Most people only dream of
And precious few have seen
I've lost all hope of rescue
I've drifted out too far
I'm doomed to spend forever
On my walk amongst the stars
My oxygen is failing
It hasn't long to go
So I may as well accept it
And enjoy the greatest show
I think about my daughter
And wave a last goodbye
When they ask her where her daddy is
She'll point up to the sky
I wonder what the future holds

As I drift here round and round
Will I orbit for eternity?
Or will I end up found?
In some ways I'm immortal
The way I die, I'll stay
The man who walked forever
Across the Milky Way.

After They've Gone

I feel a little tear appear
In the corner of my eye
As I think about the day I've had
When we said our last goodbye
People often watch you
Observing how you cope
But I was somewhere else today
I'd run right out of rope
People came and spoke to me
The things they said were kind
But they were just like distant noise
In the background of my mind
I drifted through the life we've spent
Which has nearly all been fun
You were more than half of me
And both of us were one
Now I'm sitting here alone
I asked the last to go
I had to be alone with you
And let my feelings show
That tear has grown and broken free
It's on my cheek descending
I wished I'd been a writer
I'd have wrote a better ending.

A is for 'Orses

Just bought a shy knee smart phone
It's proofed a grate new toy
Sew now I right my versus
Bye dick tatum with my voice
It e fen makes suggestive
And safe sme lots of thyme
No more type in quay boreds
I can constipate on rhyme
It even has a spiel cheque
Core rectum what I right
Fillet in my miss in words
And may king it all white
I'm now a hytec pervert
My converse shun is complete
In few char I'll wright poe ems
While stalking in the street.

Amelia

It was just a Morris Mini
Made in 1959
It was old and rather tatty
But what mattered, it was mine
But it wasn't just a motor car
It meant the world to me
It gave me liberation
'Twas the thing that set me free
I felt the need to name it
And then "Millie" came to mind
Back then it was a grannie's name
The oddest I could find
Amelia was christened
And it seemed to suit her well
The only car that had a name
As far as I could tell
I simply drove it everywhere
And it never missed a beat
Despite her ragged edges
She would not admit defeat
But slowly I grew older
And I felt the need for more
And Millie lost her lustre
She just wasn't like before
My wife now has a Mini
That is more than twice as fast
But it's somehow lost the magic
Of that old one of the past
The one thing I insist on
That will always be the same
Yes, I'm sure you've guessed it
It has got the same old name.

A Message to Michael

Mike my friend
You've let me down
You know the reason why
I had such plans for you and me
Or is it you and I?
I thought you'd live forever
You were always in my past
My future's now a hole in it
A void that's oh so vast
I doubt you'll ever read this
But how am I to tell?
This is a very public way
For me to say farewell
I can't believe I've lost you
In a moment you were gone
My constant in a changing world
I'll miss you later on
I will forgive you leaving
Though your timing rather stinks
Trust you to make an exit
At your turn to buy the drinks
I have to make a joke of it
I bet you knew I would
But if I could see you one last time
I'd buy the drinks for good
I have got other Michaels
I've got Mary, Ron and Sue
I shall hold them very tightly now
Case they go the same as you.

A Rambling

So I came across this sheepdog
Whilst walking on a track
It prevented any progress
With a very long way back
Then it suddenly turned nasty
And it tried quite hard to bite
So I summoned up a size 9 boot
And kicked with all my might
The kick was quite successful
But that moment I awoke
The wife was climbing back in bed
And couldn't see the joke.

As the Sun Sets

The shadows spread across the stones
That mark a thousand graves
An ever longer shape they make
Across the names engraved
If you haven't been to Langemark
You won't know what I mean
But the shadows of the figures there
Are a very moving scene
The fallen here are German
The dead of First World War
Whose names are in their thousands
In the shadows on the floor
The average age was twenty
Each one a mother's son
All called up by the Kaiser
And slaughtered by the gun
So spare a thought for them tonight
Just a moment would be nice
'Cos their leader chose to pick a fight
And those young men paid the price.

At the Checkout

He's standing at the checkout
The one that's number three
I spotted him so quickly
But he hasn't noticed me
Maybe I should speak to him
But I'm not sure what to say
To the boy who once meant everything
In a world that slipped away
I ponder on what might have been
But none of it makes sense
We had a love so perfect
So short-lived but intense
But youth is very fickle
So it never lasted long
I wonder where we'd be today?
If it hadn't all gone wrong
He's paid his bill and leaving
I almost feel like tears
Perhaps one day we'll meet again
In another forty years.

Barney

I'm just an army soldier
It doesn't matter whose
Just imagine me in uniform
Of any sort you choose
I'm trudging through a smashed up town
In a line of weary men
It doesn't matter where it is
It doesn't matter when
There are children playing in the street
A mix of girls and boys
They make castles out of rubble
When deprived of all their toys
A little boy approaches
His eyes are filled with fear
Who are these men in uniform?
And why are they all here?
I've nothing much to give him
But I feel the urge to give
The child is thin and hungry
I fear he may not live
Then I think of Barney
A small bear with a smile
Who comforts me in battle
And I carry all the while
I hand the soft toy to him
His face lights up with glee
It clearly means as much to him
As Barney meant to me.

Blythe Spirit

I'm sitting, dozing lazily
In my usual comfy chair
When suddenly the door bell goes
But nobody is there
I look around the garden
But, as far as I can tell
They must have done a runner
And they've closed the gate as well
Then I hear a noise upstairs
Some footsteps on the floor
And I now know who the caller was
And gently close the door
The ghost is back inside the house
That's him who's to and froing
He's supposed to enter through the wall
But he finds it heavy going
He's been to see his uncle
Who haunts houses in Turin
That was him who rang the door bell
'Cos he knows I'll let him in.

Bill's Late Mates

Arriving at the churchyard
There was no one there they knew
So they asked the man who drove the car
"Is this our mate Bill's do?"
"No, the geezer in this coffin
Is some old boy called Fred."
So having nothing else to do
They attended his instead.

Bridges

I'm not sure how I got here
But I feel I now belong
I must have got it right sometimes
And I know I got it wrong
We cross each bridge at intervals
Some rivers flow quite fast
In front of us, the future calls
In the mirror is the past
We've no idea, our destiny
Just when it comes and how
We can only own this moment
So the time to live is now.

Burgled

The wardrobe doors were open
And my clothes were on the floor
It was all so very different
It was nothing like before
My knickers had been fondled
And I'm sure they'd touched my bra
Which really isn't pleasant
When you don't know who they are
I just knew that I'd been burgled
'Cos so many things had moved
I never rang the police though
'Cos the mess was much improved.

Can't You?

You stand there where they gassed them
And you tell me you won't fight
And you cannot see a circumstance
Where killing must be right.
You think it didn't matter?
'Cos they praised a different Lord
And you shouldn't be affronted
When it happens far abroad?
You stand there where they hanged them
The posts go on in rows
Can you really not imagine?
It's beyond you I suppose
Can't you feel the misery?
Can't you sense the pain?
If you ignore the history
It'll happen all again.
A death camp's not a nice place
It was never meant to be
But it's left to show the blindest
Who have chosen not to see.

Chasing Christmas

They chase the perfect Christmas
As they rampage through the store
They all think they can buy it
In their endless quest for more
The adverts on the TV
Show a Christmas filled with glee
Folks eating GM turkey
Round a plastic Christmas tree.
Mother gets some perfume
And her husband gets a drill
Plus the kids all stare at I-Phones
Whilst their parents pay the bill
But the perfume on the TV
Is all sold for its effects
To liven up a marriage
Where a couple's gone off sex.
The drill goes in the garage
'Cos he don't know what to do
If he even had a drill bit
I would doubt he'd have a clue.
And the I-Phones now are old ones
They're considered now, old hat
In a week it will be over
And I thank the Lord for that.

Chasing Shadows

I saw you on the platform
I recognised your hair
But the train came in the station
You suddenly weren't there.
I jumped aboard a carriage
Not knowing what to do
I knew I must do something
I just have to speak to you.
The train arrived at Holborn
Your hair was in the crowd
I chased you up the stairway
As fast as folk allowed.
I saw you later cross the street
As you walked down Drury Lane
But I lost you at the corner
And were never seen again.
I've seen you, oh so often
I've seen you in my dreams
I chase you almost daily
But all in vain it seems.
I miss you every moment
And we never said goodbye
I never found out where you went
I never found out why.

Clearing the Attic

It's dark and cold and gloomy
In that space beneath the roof
You find it quite unfriendly
Almost spooky. Tell the truth
But today's the day you've chosen
Where you put aside those fears
To go and chuck the junk out
That you've stored up there for years.
There's the wooden boat that dad made
And a Betamax cassette
And a box of old mementos
That once opened, you regret.
Stacks and stacks of photos
There are albums here galore
And bit by bit you weaken
As you study what's in store
Your parents at a picnic, back in 1943
It has somehow got more meaning
Now that both have ceased to be.
Then a picture of your uncle
Wearing goggles in his plane
Today he looks much younger
When you look at him again.
Your wife when she was twenty
Looking every inch the star
You look again in wonder
At that girl atop the car.
Eventually you're broken
With your resolution through
You simply can't bear parting
With the stuff that's part of you.

Clues

Last night I heard you say his name
You said it in your dreams
In a voice you once reserved for me
But not recently it seems.
In truth, I've known for ages
That your mind has been elsewhere
By the way that you've been acting
And the time spent on your hair.
You've bought a lot of clothes of late
But it's pretty plain to see
They're nothing like you used to wear
So they're clearly not for me
The clues are only tiny
Don't mean much on their own
Like the way you sometimes whisper
When you're talking on the phone.
There's the Visa bill for petrol
In a place quite far away
And the sand that's on the carpets
Of your car the other day.
It's not a name I've heard before
You've not mentioned him, awake
But heard it said in such a way
That's pretty hard to take
You might as well come out with it
And let me know the worst
Our future has great cracks in it
And the dam's about to burst.

Coffee

He sat there with his coffee
As he viewed the falling rain
The sound of it quite rhythmic
As it bashed against the pane
The wind howled in the chimney
The precipitation hard
It was almost horizontal now
As it raced across the yard
The sky got even darker
An omnipresent grey
He simply had no answer
What to do on such a day
Picking up his laptop
He sought solace on the net
But his mind soon took a corner
On a journey of regret
He'd never fore been lonely
He had never felt such pain
So he brewed another coffee
And just sat and watched the rain.

Come Dancing

So I took up ballroom dancing
Like I've seen 'em on TV
And went and bought a spangly dress
That complimented me.
My asthma makes it rather hard
And nimble I am not
But I prance around the ballroom floor
And give it all I've got
I've gradually got better
Till I think my dancing flows
Tho I have to stop quite often
'Cos I need to blow my nose.
My sinus seems to empty
Due to spinning round and round
Plus my backless dress gets looser
Then just ends up on the ground
Now everyone avoids me
And they say I look a fool
So I just keep on dancin'
With the mirror on the wall.

Comforting Dolly

Just spotted this old photograph
From London in the Blitz
With some little girl's expression
By her house all blown to bits.
But it could be taken anywhere
It's still happening today
The rich engage in struggles
And it's the poor who have to pay
Meet Miss "Collateral Damage"
With those sad and doleful eyes
She's a pseudonym for suffering
And the truth behind the lies.
It's all about self interest
It's the same the whole world through
Just a giant game of chess to them
Using weapons bought by you.
Don't look to me for answers
On how to make it cease
I just see a haunting photo
And hope the subject
Found some peace.

Coming of Night

The setting sun sinks lower
Casting shadows cross the mere
The birds are falling silent
As this winter night draws near.
The frost is now returning
Gripping everything in sight
What warmth there was departing
With the coming of the night.
A distant owl starts hooting
Through the mist across the field
He calls in expectation
What the coming night might yield.
The rabbits now retire
To their burrows underground
The world has fallen silent
Just nocturnals creep around.
The moon divides the darkness
With its shafts of silver grey
Whilst mother nature's creatures
Wait the coming of the day.

Dad

Three children building castles
In the summer by the sea
Our world was full of laughter
That's what father meant to me
A man of gentle humour
Knotted hankie on his head
He'd tease us and torment us
When he'd lie there playing dead
He'd sit there in his deck chair
Watch his children laugh with glee
We had fun with little money
That's what father meant to me
We'd go there on a steam train
On our journey to the stars
We'd walk there from the station
There was little cash for cars
A man of great compassion
Rescued Germans from the sea
They were other men in trouble
That's what father meant to me
I will have to stop this poem
It is hurting. Can't you see?
My father was my everything
That's what he meant to me.

Dance with me

I'd grab a plane to be with you
But I never get the chance
So till I'm home in three months time
Will you join me in this dance?
So take my hand and dance with me
Although we're far apart
And in my thoughts I'll dance with you
And hold you in my heart
I know that you can hear me
Because you can read my mind
We don't need a phone to speak
Our souls are so entwined
So put your arm around my back
And waltz me round the floor
And I'll dance around the room with you
Then we'll dance around some more
Now I can feel you hold me
Although you're far away
Your hand is clutching mine so tight
And I know that you're okay
Your head's now on my shoulder
And everything's alright
I'm glad they picked a slow one
Let's dance away the night.

Death of a Department Store

The keen had got there early
Whilst the rest had queued for miles
And the staff now looked despondent
Where before they'd been all smiles.
The place was being ransacked
As the greedy went to town
It was "quick, I wanna bargain
That's all mine, now tear it down"
My wife looked on horror
As the store she loved got cleared
Whilst the place was slowly dying
As each item disappeared.
I said we had to leave now
I could clearly read her mind
It was as we reached the corner
She then said and looked behind,
"Our lives are made of little things
Though quite small, they touch your heart
And it's better not to witness
When those things get torn apart."

Evening Star

The morning sun is glinting
Your paint is bright and new
I doubt you miss the freedom
Of a world you never knew.
Not for you the open track
The thrill of going fast
Scrapped before you started
Of steam, you were the last.
To some you're just an engine
A huge great lump of steel
But steam was never like that
They seemed to be quite real.
P'raps one day, they'll use you
When cars are in the past
And you will see the open sky
And have your day at last.

Everyone's a Whinny

My wife would love a rocking horse
They make her dewy eyed
A fantasy
From nursery
She carries round inside
Problem is, they cost a lot
And I really haven't got it
So I've saddled up a clothes horse
And just hope she doesn't spot it.

Finding Mrs Wright

My first wife used to nag me
She really went to town
She's buried in the garden
But only two feet down.
The second was a stunner
She was blonde and rather tall
But I found her much too flirty
So she's bricked up in the wall.
The third was rather plainer
But complained how much I drank
She's up there in a suitcase
Behind the water tank.
The fourth one is the nicest
As far as I can tell
But it seems we have no future
'Cos she moans about the smell.

Fixes

My mummy lived for fixes
Whilst my daddy did his best
To love his three small children
Plus a junkie and the rest.
I watched him slowly failing
Till one day he couldn't cope
When he sat and told us tearfully
That he'd run right out of rope.
At that time the doorbell rang
And some strangers took the boys
They could take the clothes they stood in
But must leave behind their toys.
I ran and hugged my daddy
And I asked how could this be?
And then again the doorbell went
This time they came for me.
That evening with the strangers
I screamed "This isn't fair!"
And was told I should be grateful
I was taken into "care".
My daddy's hugs were over
All the love I'd get, was had
I'd just become a number
In a system with no dad.

Fizz the Magic Dragon

Just bumped into a dragon
And he didn't look too bright
He asked if I could help him
'Cos his burner wouldn't light.
It appears he'd fallen in a pond
And his igniter'd got all wet
Never met one on a walk before
Nor have you...I bet.

Grains of sand

I sometimes see an hour glass
I see it in my dreams
The sand is slowly running through
It drops each day it seems.
I've seen it now for many years
And watched the grains of sand
But now it's getting really low
I wonder what's at hand.
I fear that it portends my fate
My future now looks short
Or should I turn it upside down?
Now there's a tempting thought.

Happy Landings?

"Excuse me, can you tell me
Why we're flying round and round?
I sometimes see the sea down there
And sometimes see the ground"
"All that I can tell you sir,
We have a problem with the plane
Now would you keep your voice down please
And don't mention it again."
Robbie sat there in his seat
And felt himself perspire
And started looking round about
For any signs of fire.
Then the Captain gave a message
In which he summoned all the crew
It must have been a meeting
Where he told them what to do.
Robbie felt the need for air
And now felt rising fear
Then he heard the Captain's voice
Say what no one wants to hear
"We seem to have a problem..
The landing gear has jammed
We will now divert to London
And we'll not proceed as planned"
The message met with silence
Till a woman starts to cry
As each and everyone on board
Starts to wonder if they'll die.
The plane then starts its slow descent
And jerks from side to side
As the Captain tries to free the wheels

They need so badly for the ride.
Then Robbie sees the runway
And really gets a fright
The whole field's full of vehicles
And a thousand flashing lights.
Almost every fire engine
For fifty miles around
Was sitting waiting patiently
For when they hit the ground
The plane then made an impact
With something like a groan
And they bumped along
Quite noiselessly
On a massive bed of foam
Then at last it came to stop
And the crew all start to shout:
"COME ON! GET YOUR BELTS UNDONE
WE REALLY MUST GET OUT!"

Her Poem Bites Back

The poem was a sad one
She had written for a friend
Which was somehow much more poignant
Being read out at her end.
She wished she hadn't written it
Hadn't made it quite so sad
But was upset when she wrote it
And had given all she had.
The ending was the worst bit
And she knew she'd shed some tears
As she struggled for composure
In the face of all her peers.
Line by line it worsened
As the dreaded end came nigh
And the line that made her struggle
When at last she said goodbye.
Then suddenly it's over
And the reader takes her leave
She had made it without howling
And allowed herself to breathe.

Hindsight

If you could have your time again
What changes would you make?
Would you take another course
Not make the same mistake?
Looking back it's easy
To know where you went wrong
But have you landed in the place
In truth, that you belong?
Changing one thing on the way
Would only make one change
You'd then be on your own again
And everything's then strange
You cannot live life backwards
Correcting as you go
The devil's still the devil
Are they best
The ones you know?

Hooray!

No doubt we'll all be counting down
As the magic time draws near
And cheering at the prospect
Of another brand new year
We somehow feel ourselves renewed
At the striking of the chimes
And think a change of number
Will lead to better times
Forgetting how the last one
Had turned out just the same
As all those that preceded
We'd cheered that when it came
But I will no doubt join you
Get drunk and play the fool
Cheering in that brand new year
Where nothing changed at all.

"Hope I Die, Before I Get Old"

"Now Robbie, you be careful"
Her plea to me absurd
'Cos I was just a teenage boy
And never heard a word.
Standing at the window
My mother watched me go
As I roared off on my scooter
To where, she didn't know
When young you are invincible
There is little that you fear
Thoughts of peers mean everything
That's all that you hold dear
Riding round in packs of boys
We raced around the town
In an endless game of "chicken"
Then one of us went down.
The car had pulled in front of him
And Ronnie met his end
I wonder where he is today?
My skinhead scooter friend.

Ignition

There's nothing good about it
It's just another day
Of peering through a window
At a world that's dull and grey
You feel the need to go to town
But not to paint it red
But another day spent all alone
You might as well be dead.
So you end up in a tea shop
'Cos you feel you want to eat
But there's no one sitting with you
'Cos there's no one else to meet.
Then a woman in the corner
Does somehow catch your eye
And with nothing else of interest
You watch her by and by.
She's not some raving beauty
Just a woman 'bout your age
She's reading some old paperback
And you watch her turn the page.
So you try and read the menu
And force yourself to look
But your eyes keep drifting up again
At that woman with the book.
There's a feeling deep inside you
That started with a spark
It's slowly getting brighter
And it brightens up your dark.

That woman has a countenance
That's somehow got you caught

And you find her more of interest
Than all the food you bought.
Then all your dreams get shattered
As she leaves and goes to pay
But she's done you quite a favour
'Cos she's brightened up your day.

Imagine This

Life is not a bowl of cherries
Ignore what's in the song
It's not a bowl of things at all
The song you see, is wrong
Think of it as rhubarb
And don't forget the custard
A mixture of the sharp and sweet
And a word to say when flustered.

I'm Being Called

There's a house occurring in my dreams
Ever since I saw it
I feel it wants to meet me
And I simply can't ignore it.
Been standing there five centuries
Since 1482
From an age before the Tudors
So what am I to do?
Is there something bad in there?
An ogre from the past?
Or was I there in former life
And must return to it at last?

I've decided I must call upon
That house that brings me fright
I must confront my demons
Or I'll never sleep at night.
So I'm standing at the iron gates
And view with trepidation
The prospect of arrival there
Don't fill me with elation.
So I set off very briskly
And walk along the drive
But the nearer that I get to it
The less I do arrive.
It's like I'm on a treadmill
But nothing's going round
I find I make no progress
And cannot turn around.
It's like a living nightmare
And I'm getting really cold
The scenery is changing

And my clothes are getting old.
Next thing I'm aware of
There's a chain around my throat
And I'm looking out a window
From a house inside a moat.
It's clear the house has claimed me
But why it isn't clear
Perhaps I'll find the reason
From those voices I do hear?

"The Yorkists will rejoice tonight
When they hear the news we bring
Now we've caught the last descendant
Of the man who killed the King"

Inner Peace

The shingle roars in sequence
With the timing of the surf
As the waves ad infinitum
Come crashing down to earth
The human race is absent
Not a single ship to see
Just me and mother nature
The epitome of free
The air is full of seaspray
On a brisk refreshing breeze
You can't not feel life's wonderful
On summer days like these.

Inside a Dream

Last night I woke and in the room
A scene appeared from out the gloom
How it got there, I know not
T'was of a Christmas long forgot
A bombed out street, a dismal scene
An ancient house, near Bethnal Green
The roof all creaked with weight of snow
Winter's meant it, long ago
There's Grandma, Bruvver, Mum and Me
Whilst father fixed the Christmas tree
Nan was farting rather loud
Enough to make a trooper proud
She blamed it on the sprouts she'd had
But this attack was really bad
Mother left to make some tea
She weren't that keen on farts, you see
Dad ignored her, fixed the lights
Ol' nan when farting, weren't best sights
Big bruvver loved it, sat and grinned
The thought of grandma breaking wind
Then nan jumped up and quick departed
I think she may have more than farted
The scene is now a great less clear
It's fading fast, I'm back right here
Just in time, the lights come on
Dad had fixed 'em, now it's gone.

...is Bliss

The passengers alighted
It was great to leave the plane
Two weeks to come in Malta
'Fore they have to fly again
Everyone's excited
As the weather is a dream
Mum and dads are smiling
You should hear the children scream
Grabbing every suitcase
Least the ones that look like theirs
The kids go search for buses
As their dad puffs up the stairs
The pilot views them leaving
Thanking God they never guessed
That the plane that he just landed
Had a minute's fuel at best.

Is Stat You?

I think I need an Ethos
Like the one in Piccadilly
He's got a bow and arrow
And he frankly looks quite silly.
My Ethos would be rounder
More akin to Rupert Bear
At least I'd have a scarf on
Not standing there
All bare.

Is There Anybody There?

To you, I'm just a brussel sprout
That's sticking out the stalk
But if you listen really hard
Don't ya know that we can talk?
No one ever listens
They just chuck us in to cook
But we have all got eyes and ears
If they'd only stop and look
We only have a tiny voice
And you have to be quite near
So next time you're in the grocer's
Stick a brussel in yer ear.

I've Come Here to the Hospital

To see a girl I know
But passing such a sad old man
I stop to say hello.
"How are you?" I ask him
His eyes look far away
I'm sure that where his mind is now
It's nicer than today.
Is he in some golden time?
With his sweetheart in the scene
Dreaming of the things he's done
In the places that he's been
Or perhaps he sees a sunset?
As it merges with the sea
Somewhere in some far off place
Which means more to him, than me
Perhaps he finds great comfort
In the places he holds dear
A time and place of choosing
That is better there than here.
Then he looks me in the eye
His eyes are green like mine
I begin to feel uneasy
And I shiver down my spine.
Now I see his name tag
It's a name that I know well
The date is in the future
But it's far too blurred to tell
I now see what I witness
It's the me of future years
It's not what I expected
And beyond my greatest fears.

Lambretta

It doesn't get much better
Though I'm trying to forget her
That girl on that Lambretta
Stole my heart.
But my feelings just got fonder
As she disappeared off yonder
But I couldn't get my Honda
Bike to start.
So I'll admit defeat
It's not partial, it's complete
'Cos I'll never get to meet
That work of art.
Now I've ceased to be a suitor
I imagine that'll suit her
An' I 'ope her rotten scooter
Falls apart.

Last Rights

"My darling I am sorry"
She whispered in my ear
Her voice now fading quickly
It was all I could to hear.
"I know I was a bad choice
And I played you for a fool
That you kept forgiving
I did not deserve at all.
I left you with the children
And you took it on the chin
Your patience seemed quite endless
Yet it must have worn quite thin."
Her eyes became wide open
As she lay there creased in pain
Our time together short now
Time we'd never have again...
"My darling, you relax now
Don't apologise to me
It's why I had to kill you
Put that arsenic in your tea."

Life's Too Short

"Robbie will you stay behind?"
The teacher said in class
"Your silly pranks and comic lines
Just make my class
A FARCE!"
But then his tone relented
It had seemed I touched a nerve
His voice took on a wistful tone
As he slowly lost reserve.
"Robbie, go and have your fun
Enjoy it while you can
The world will take its toll on you
And you'll soon become a man.
Then life is never quite the same
Like it is for you today
The pressures seem to grow in size
And the fun gets squeezed away.
Boyhood is a precious thing
You only get one chance
So grab it while you can, my son
And lead us all a dance."

Love Reins O'er Me

I look into her dark brown eyes
We share each other's gaze
We have the perfect friendship
In oh so many ways.
She loves me 'cos I feed her
And she listens to my woes
She never interrupts me
However long it goes.
People come and people go
They rarely stay the course
Don't bother with a dating site
Go get yourself an 'orse.

Low Life!

The wardrobe doors were open
And my clothes were on the floor
It was all so very different
It was nothing like before
My knickers had been fondled
And I'm sure they'd touched my bra
Which really isn't pleasant
When you don't know who they are
I just knew that I'd been burgled
'Cos so many things had moved
I never rang the police though
'Cos the mess was much improved.

Manifestly Wrong

I've haunted you for ages
And it clearly isn't fair
That I should stand behind you
When you try to do your hair.
Our love will last forever
And I know you hold me dear
But it's time I think I left you
So I'll slowly disappear.
Don't look at me so sadly
You're alive and young and free
You need to find another now
Not a manifest like me.
I'll visit when you're sleeping
When you're tucked up in your bed
So we can be together
In the safety of your head.
You can opt out if you want to
It's as easy as it seems
But I'll always come and hold you
If you call me in your dreams.

Meeting of Minds...

I've a note here in my diary
I'm invited to attend
A meeting with the folk I knew
From London's old East End.
There'll be lots and lots of laughter
And no doubt lots of tears
All holding hands across a bridge
To a time they shared with peers.
But I'd rather leave it all to them
I think I'll stop at home
They can't see what I can see
So it's better left alone.
The venue is the problem
It's the pub I spent my youth
The place is full of ghosts for me
It scares me, tell the truth
There'll be far more folk attending
Than the organisers know
And the pub will end up heaving
With the folk who live below.
So I think I'll just forget it
Leave the sleeping dogs to lie
It's the faces in the corners
That would make me want to cry.

Mutual Destruction

When I think of what I did
And the things I said to you
And how we both all messed it up
'Cos we weren't sure what to do
The sniping and the bitterness
And those pointless retributions
All those kinder things I didn't say
To bring 'bout restitution.
It was mostly said in anger
To even up the score
But the spring just wound up tighter
And we both hit back with more.
Most of it I didn't mean
I just wanted it to hurt
That's all you ever think of
When it comes to throwing dirt.
I often wonder how you are
You're still there in my heart
If only we'd been older then
We'd be wiser from the start.

Missed Shot

I only have one picture
Of her standing by the sea
Now each pixel has more value
Than a private jet to me
I need to get it printed
Make it bigger, six foot tall
So I'll see her every morning
Standing framed against the wall
I wish now I'd took dozens
Of our favourite beauty spot
With her standing looking gorgeous
In the smartest clothes she'd got
But I've only got this picture
In her jeans and tousled hair
With her standing on the clifftop
Then she's suddenly not there...

My Country

I've often thought I must be mad
I've lost so many friends
I know my luck is getting short
And we all know how it ends.
But every time I fly above
This land I see below
I never wonder why I'm here
It's my country and I know.

Based on the words of a Spitfire pilot in 1940

My Daughter

If only I could touch you
But I can only wait
And listen to your feeble heart
With its rapid, pulsing, rate
Your little tiny eyes are closed
You barely move at all
I said I'd swap my life for yours
If I ever got the call
The other babes have been and gone
They came and went real fast
But I can only sit and watch
My daughter through the glass.
Why was she born so feeble?
Was it something we did wrong?
I'm told we'll have to wait and see
But why's it take so long?
It's all I ever wanted
A daughter of my own
And she's stuck inside a plastic box
So very much alone.

Nightfall

The guns had fallen silent
As the dark replaced the day
And Gerry started singing
To his foe across the way
The sound of choral voices
Seemed to drift across the void
That piece of Mother Planet
That was utterly destroyed.
And Tommy sang an answer
It was flat and made no sense
But Gerry still applauded
They'd no wish to cause offence.
The starlight spread like silver
As the Earth begat the Moon
The frosty ground was solid
Come the time to end the tune.
The human spirit conquered
Like old friends they called "Good night!"
Tomorrow would come shortly
And they'd carry on the fight.

On-line Love

Tonight's the night I meet her
That girl from off the net
My stomach's really out of sorts
How nervous can you get?
I wish I'd been more honest now
Not told so many lies
I never thought I'd meet her though
Now lying wasn't wise.
My picture was an old one
Before my hair went grey
I dare say when she sees me
She'll just turn and walk away.
Whilst her picture's like a film star
As glamorous can be
Why she ain't got lots of men
Is the thing that bothers me.
Why did I pretend so much?
I'm just an ordinary guy
Now I've gone and blown it all
By starting with a lie.
I don't want to date a film star
Men stare at in the street
I just want a nice sweet girl
But they seem so hard to meet.

On the Gallows

I'm standing on the gallows
As the man adjusts the rope
I was hoping my reprieve had come
But I've now run out of hope
You know I never killed her
Those police they sent were blind
All I did was move the knife
And left my fingerprints behind.
I saw the man who did it
Before he ran away
He was standing in the court, you know
When they sentenced me that day.
I tried so hard to save her
I gave her CPR
That's how I got the blood on me
And why it went so far.
But now the day I dread has come
The day that seals my fate
And just to make the whole thing worse
My tax return is late.

On Tick

The clock has started ticking
But so what? I'm Mr Cool
That's the last screw on the cover
And my hands don't shake at all
This bomb is pretty massive
'Bout my weight in TNT
And unless I work real quickly
It's goodbye to little me
The streets around are emptied
Just the Police behind the screens
'Cept for me inside this car bomb
Who gets blown to smithereens
Now disconnect that trembler
Let's be really quiet please
Not the slightest little movement
Oh my God. I'm gonna sneeze...

Out Shopping

A woman standing next to me
Reached forward for a pot
But the voice of someone with her said
"That's more than we have got"
What's happened to the world today
When you can't afford some jam?
And I'm left feelin' guilty
Just because I can
My first thought was to "buy it them"
But my second one was "no"
It could sound quite insulting
From a man they didn't know
I didn't want their gratitude
Or a single word of thanks
But it wasn't me who broke the world
T'was those clever sods in banks.

Orses Doofers.

Took my pony to the vets today
'Cos he seemed a little hoarse
The vet said he was really old
"'Cos those teeth he's got are false"
You know, everything I ever do
Is a list of misadventures
Now I've bought a horse so old
It's got a set of dentures.

Panda to me

When I'm looking in the mirror
I appear the wrong way round
Which doesn't seem to matter much
As far as I have found
But it must cause certain problems
When make-up you apply
How do ladies put mascara on
When they've only got one eye?

Passing Kiss

I was blown a kiss today
By a woman as she passed
I'm walking, she is driving
So it happened really fast.
My day till then, a bad one
So I'm feeling rather low
But then I saw this gesture
From a woman that I know.
Love is all around us
It's a basic human need
And she did it though she meant it
That simple fleeting deed.
My day somehow got brighter
Made the bad things all rescind
When I felt the work of magic
Of a kiss upon the wind.

Past caring

I'd planned to have some sex last night
Not had some for a while
The thought of it quite cheered me up
It even made me smile
But we'd just got past the pillow talk
And the wife did start to doze
So that's my chance for this year gone
I've blown it I suppose.

Peanuts

The first time that I kissed her
It just all went down the pan
I don't think she was ready
So it didn't go to plan.
We'd both been eating peanuts
So the kiss was rather dry
She also tasted salty
So I guess that might be why.
We'd been dancing at a party
I had picked her from the crowd
Though talking wasn't easy
With the music on so loud.
She really was a dancer
Whereas I had two left feet
A hopeless sense of rhythm
And a worse still sense of beat.
I was better with the slow ones
It was good to hold her near
Until I tried to light up
Which she grabbed and dowsed with beer.
"I came here wearing perfume
And you'll make me smell of smoke.
If you must smoke when you're dancing
Go and and find yourself a bloke."
I felt a little stupid
But this girl was full of spark
So I held her even tighter
As we're dancing in the dark.
Then suddenly she vanished
She just said she had to go
And she left me at a party
With some folk I didn't know.

Thanking them and leaving
With no dancing girl in sight
I went and found my motor
On that chill and foggy night.
She was standing at a bus stop
As I drove along the street
Looking lost and rather lonely
And quite scared of who'd she meet.
We chatted as I drove her
And I stopped outside her door
The second kiss was perfect
So much better than before.

Perfection

I stopped and looked a moment
At the beauty of the sky
A majesty of blueness
Not a single cloud drifts by
It's the kind of simple thing
That we rarely feast our eyes on
A canopy so everyday
That goes to all horizons
I doubt that in the universe
There's greater sight to see
It's more than just a roof you know
It's the reason that we be.

Perverts

I went to get the washing in
And came back with a frown
My underwear
Was everywhere
All strewn upon the ground.
A crime had been committed
Both insulting and unkind
They had gone and stole me clothes pegs
And they'd left me knix behind.

Poems

Poetry is boring
'Tis a thing that people say
Two lines and they're distracted
And with four, they walk away.
"It's a thing for toffs and fairies
I don't get it, can't you see?
All that romance and beauty
Are completely lost on me."
Then one day in a crisis
With their backs against the wall
Someone reads a little poem
And it wasn't crap at all.

Putting Things Right

There's never been a verse I've seen
Devoted to the scrotum
They're not a thing you write about
So no one's ever wrote 'em
But people write of other parts
And often go to town
But never mention testicles
It must really get them down.
They're not a thing of beauty
As a spectacle, they're not
But your only 'ere because of one
It's not fair, that they're
Forgot.

Rain

The rain now falls relentlessly
Ends weeks of heat and drought
The water rushing everywhere
And pouring roundabout
It's splashing out the drainpipes
Making lakes upon the floor
Water, water everywhere
Where none had been before
The flowers can't believe it
The lawn is quite awash
The drought it seems has ended
In one almighty splosh.

Riches

The formula was simple
Three children round a tree
It was only very basic
But it meant the world to me.
The decs were made of paper
Subtle, they were not
We'd made them round the table
Using anything we'd got.
The lights were old and dodgy
They'd flicker and they'd blow
And Dad would spend half Christmas day
Just getting them to go.
The gifts were inexpensive
But the room was filled with joy
T'was a season full of magic
Was my Christmas as a boy.
I look back now with fondness
At those times that I recall.
I now know I had riches
And I wasn't poor at all.

Scratched Love

The poem on the window made
On a rainy summer's day
Has long outlived its writer
And won't ever fade away
'Bout love that's unrequited
That has made him so forlorn
The lady who's the subject
Gone an age fore I was born.
His sentiments are timeless
That are scratched here on the glass
A message from a lover
That has lasted from the past.
The world is ever changing
Things he knew are gone for good
But some things last forever
And for always understood.

Second Thoughts

The night is getting colder
The mist it cloaks the ground
And now a silent breeze awakes
And moves it all around.
A barn owl calls across the fields
Prompting answers from the wood
Including one, quite loudly
From almost where I'm stood.
The great bird's call alarms me
It must have known I'm here
I start to think this silly prank
Was not a good idea.
I was playing with a ouija board
It was just a silly game
When suddenly it came to life
And asked for me by name.
This spirit asked to meet me
And suggested we meet here
A silent place in daytime
At night engenders fear.
A twig breaks right behind me
It's dark and moves unseen
Then I stare in utter terror
At the face of Halloween.

Seeking the Past

He was old and very wrinkled
He just sat there in his chair
All but time ignored him
No one cared that he was there
He had never had a visit
He was left there quite alone
There was no one left to visit now
Or call him on the phone
His eyesight slowly failing
He was slowly going blind
But in the dark behind those eyes
He existed in his mind
Inside he was a young man
His hair was blond with curls
A body full of muscles
And a favourite with the girls
His life was full of pleasure
He was young and fancy free
Looking quite the film star
In his racing green MG
The chair in which he sat in
And his empty life today
Was somewhere in the future
And a million miles away.

Self Catering

I've been left to do my dinner
'Cos my wife is feeling ill
So I'm boiling up a Quiche Lorraine
And got baked beans in the grill.
I thought I'd do a poached egg
But it don't look like it oughta
Now the poacher's gone misshapen
'Cos I left out all the water.
The smoke alarm is going mad
The wife's screaming from her bed-
I'll slide off down the pub I think
And 'ave pie and chips instead.

Shadows

I turned around and glimpsed my past
The whole of Memory Lane
I saw my friends and called their names
But alas it was in vain
T'was just their shadows fading fast
I'll not turn round again.

Shouldering It

He was standing at the check out
With his trolley full of stuff
Someone tapped him on the shoulder
Said "You sure you got enough?"
She only had three items
And her child was dressed in rags
And he had got such shopping
It would barely fit in bags.
Ignoring her, he packed it all
And paid it on his card
But something really troubled him
'Cos he really weren't that hard.
Then as the woman left the shop
He gave her all he'd bought
He forced her hand to take it
Said she'd given him much thought.
Then walking off with nothing
He just left her where she stood
He had drunk the Christmas spirit
And he suddenly felt good.

Starlight

The stars are so dramatic
The most beautiful of sights
The jewels bedeck the heavens
On this darkest of all nights.
The silence all but deafens
It is utter and profound
I am drifting into dreamland
On this total lack of sound.
I dream of sunny schooldays
As I wander through my past
The friends who stayed forever
And the ones that didn't last.
My mind is slowly drifting
As I ponder through my days
The colours slowly fading
To a palette full of greys.
The cold is taking over
But it hurts less than I feared
It now seems like forever
Since Titanic disappeared.

Sunrise

It started as suggestion
A reduction of the dark
But it was so, so early
Before the keenest Lark.
Then the sky began to lighten
From just black it turned to grey
And we were left in no doubt now
Of the coming of the day
The greyness turned to colour
The sky a sort of blue
Whilst the grass and trees around me
Did take on every hue.
Then a tiny golden line appeared
It was just above the sea
Which stirred up lines of poetry
From the inner depths of me.
The golden light did cast its glow
To the heavens in great rays
A sight to see so beautiful
Will be with me all my days
The sun was on its journey
To the summit of the sky
I was left in utter wonder
At the scene before my eyes.
At last the sun had cleared the sea
The day had now begun
And behind me sang a Blackbird
To greet the morning sun.

Superted

I've always had my "Superted"
I cuddle him when I'm in bed.
His head came off when I was three
He's not far off as old as me
But Mummy sewed him safe and sound
Shame it's on the wrong way round
He's had new eyes so he can see
But they're not where they used to be.
One ear's off, the other's loose
S'pose that comes from too much use.
His squeak fell out the other year
I store it with his other ear.
His pads are thin
He lost his nose
When he and Golly came to blows
But Ted and I've seen thick and thin
Which might explain the shape he's in.
Maybe "Super" doesn't suit him any more
But he is quite big at six foot four.

Sweetie Pie

She used to call me "Sweetie Pie"
A name I used to hate
And she'd often say it loudly
In the earshot of my mates.
She'd talk about my underpants
To any girl that calls
'Bout the last thing that I needed
Was a chat about my "smalls".
She would sing me Happy Birthday
Down the speaker phone at work
So I would curl up cringing
Whilst the blokes all went berserk.
She would wave her arms and "Cooeee!"
If she saw me in the street
So I'd often dive up alleys
In an effort not to meet.
My mother couldn't help it
To embarrass was her way
And what I'd give to hear her
Call out "Sweetie Pie" today.

Tail End

I stroke you really slowly
My dear and faithful friend
All curled up in your basket
We both know it's the end.
You lit my days with sunshine
On days it never shone
You'll always be remembered
Long after you have gone.
You've been my "soul" companion
Your love for me is plain
If I could turn the clock back
We'd do it all again.

Telling Her

I had barely crossed the threshold
And had not yet closed the door
When my daughter's in the hallway
And demands to know the score
I had vowed I wouldn't tell her
I had wanted her be spared
But my acting skills were hopeless
She could tell that I was scared
So I told her very gently
All the good bits barely true
But the punch line couldn't alter
There was nothing they could do
Then I watched her slowly crumble
As she sank upon her knees
Her big eyes looking upward
In a pair of visual pleas
The news completely changed her
I could hear it in her cries
Her childhood had left her
I could see it in her eyes.

That Girl on the Train...

She was hid behind her paper
She was so behind "The Times"
She would hiss her indignation
Bout the news of certain crimes
Her legs and hair were gorgeous
Not a strand was out of place
But the broadsheet hid her from me
I could never glimpse her face
At last I had to stand up
As my destination neared
So sadly disappointing
When I saw she had a beard.

The Bank Account

Queueing at the food bank
She could feel she'd shed a tear
As she pondered on her losses
Like her house, her pride, career.
Where once she'd go out shopping
And return with Chloé skirts
She now stood in a back street
With the shame so bad, it hurt.
The girl who'd live to party
Who'd had breakfast with champagne
Such heady days had vanished
And she'd not see them again.
First the fancy job went
And the house to clear the debts
Then shallow friendships crumbled
Leaving nothing but regrets.
Just a life sustained by food banks
That were there to feed the poor
The ones she'd walked by, drinking
Smelling unwashed on the floor.
And now she found she'd joined them
Her humbling complete
It's amazing how you stumble
When you've nothing much to eat.

The Bubble

Thank you for your interest
And I'm flattered that you care
But I'm living in the past, you see
And I'm still quite happy there.
My world is in her shadow
And it's not a pretty sight
When I speak to her in daytime
And I hold her hand each night.
I make the tea each morning
And I make enough for two
I only need a tea bag now
But it's more than I can do.
Maybe in the future
Not sure when but later on
I'll find the need for new love
When I've come to terms, she's gone.
Till then I'm in a bubble
Which I'm much too scared to burst
I cannot start a new life
Till I've put to bed the first.

The Bus to Flanders

The ancient bus crawled up the hill
And stopped where I was waiting
I jumped on board quite gratefully
As the wait had been frustrating.
It was only once I'd got on board
That I found things out of place
There were other folk upon the bus
But none who had a face.
Everyone was dressed in green
And all of them were men
No one spoke a single word
'Cept for moaning now and then.
I was never asked for money
The ride it seems, was free
In an endless line of buses
As far as I could see.
In a state of rising panic
I tried to ring the bell
Then the man who sat beside me said
"It won't stop till you get there son
It's all aboard for hell."

The Call

Simon put the phone down
And he stood there deep in thought
Quite shattered by the impact
Of the news that call had brought.
The life he'd known had ended
Now not the same at all
His comfort zone quite shattered
By a thirty second call.
The children sensed disaster
All now ceased to play
They stood and watched their father
And wondered what he'd say.
The youngest made a whimper
So his brother took his hand
This was not the time for antics
It was time to make a stand.
"Daddy what's the matter?"
His eldest asked with fear
Who sensed a coming answer
That she didn't want to hear.
Paternal instinct rallied
Simon had to hold the line
He turned and hugged his daughter
"Don't you fret now, we'll be fine."

The Chain

I've got my grandad's humour
And my grannie's light green eyes
And speak just like my father
Which I s'pose is no surprise.
My suntan is a throwback
From a forebear, once from Spain
It misses generations
Then surfaces again.
We are the products of our past
All handed down the line
Our tiny flaws and facets
Adjusting all the time.
Do you ever round a corner
And you know just what's in store?
You're a tiny part of grandad
Who'd walked that way before.

The Decanter

Time hasn't moved so slowly
For twenty years or more
Since watching that decanter
Descending to the floor.
It happened in slow motion
As the antique neared the ground
I cringed in expectation
Of the coming, crashing, sound.
It exploded like a hand grenade
When at last the falling stopped.
Don't juggle with decanters
They're bound to end up dropped.

The Dim and Distant Past

Before we had computers
We learnt typing from the start
And you whizzed round with the Tippex
When you misspelt part with fart
And if you really, really typed too fast
The type bars jammed together
One shot out the window once
And disapp ard for v r
And it had to b th " "
That disapp ard from sight
Which mak s trying to finish this po m off
So bloody hard to writ .

The Door

There is a door in my old house
And I don't know where it goes
There can't be much behind it
Just a cupboard I suppose.
I've tried so hard to open it
But it seems I'm out of luck
That door's been shut a hundred years
So it's well and truly stuck.
I've kicked it and I've pushed it
Like the police do on TV
But though that seems to work for them
It clearly don't for me
Last night I had another go
To see what I could learn
But before I even touched it
The knob began to turn.
I backed away in terror
As the knob went to and fro
Then quickly slid the bolts across
As fast as they would go
I don't care what's behind it
But it must be understood
You can tease me if you want to
But that door stays shut
For good.

The Early Bird

"I beg your pardon"
I said in the garden
To the Blackbird
Right under my fork

Then with coat black as coal
He dived in a hole
And emerged with a triumphant squawk

The worm was a squiggle
And starting to wriggle
But was gripped in his beak, like a vice

Then without any sound
It started on down
And there it was gone, in a trice.

The Enigma

Thought I'd write a verse or two
And use a sort of code
So I bought an old "Enigma"
From a bloke just down the road
It's full of plugs and rotas
And I can't read what comes out
Trouble is, I've no idea
What my poem was about.

The End

I knew that day her time had come
She spent so long asleep
It was not the gentle dreaming kind
Her slumber was so deep.
She woke and said "I'm tired"
That was all she had to say
Then slowly right in front of me
She gently slipped away
At first I thought she slumbered
But her breath I could not see
She was off to meet her destiny
Wherever that may be.

The End of the Twirl

Ballet school has dumped me
'Cos my demi-pointe's gone blunt
And my chassé is deformé
As it tends to 'ang out front.
My ballon's rather heavy
And my dessous is a flop
And when I do a piqué turn
Then it's kinda hard to stop.
My pirouette is passé
And my jetés banged to rights
But just to put it bluntly
I look pretty shit in tights.

The Ghost of Christmas Yet to Come?

My ancient house is playing tricks
Or there're others live between its bricks
'Cos I often feel I'm not alone
And the noise I hear is not my own.
There's sometimes someone next to me
But who she is, I cannot see
I'm told it's just imagination
But I swear I hear her conversation.

But it isn't me she's talking to
So there're others here that aren't in view
In the early hours, she's rather clearer
As though the gap between us
Gets much nearer
And I sometimes hear our third stair creaking
Along with ghostly laughs and distant speaking.

But the clothes she wears are rather queer
Which brings me to my greatest fear
That the time she's in, is yet to be
Which makes me the one who's history
And that's the part that scares me most
Perhaps she's quite real and I'm the ghost?

I've got to go, she seems disturbed
As though she's heard my every word
I'm scared to write another line
'Cos her eyes are staring straight at mine.

The Ghost of Parham Airfield

On a long forgotten runway
All cracked an' going green
I can hear approaching engines
Of a Boeing Seventeen.
'Twas brought here from Seattle
In nineteen forty four
Flown each and every mission
It only had one more
Then on that final journey
They were on the homeward run
When suddenly a One Oh Nine
Attacked it out the sun
But no one saw it tumble
It vanished in thin air
That's the plane that's coming now
Behind me, over there.
'Tis the ghost of Parham Airfield
It plays on people's fears
The never ending mission
That will last a thousand years.
Now I'm the one who hears it
That bomber from the past
I sometimes go and wait for it
'Case it makes it back at last.

The Girl in Blue

I was sitting drinking coffee
As I'd suffered quite a blow
My company was shrinking
I was told I had to go.
The coffee shop was crowded
And with nothing much to do
Eyes rested on a pretty girl
Who was sat there, wearing blue.
Then staring at my coffee
'Cos it tasted rather vile
Looking up, she'd vanished
Left her brief case in the aisle.
I picked it up to chase her
Do my good deed for the day
But the outside street was crowded
And I wasn't sure which way.
Then I saw her in the distance
And pursued the girl in blue
Having once been in the army
I then stuck to her like glue.
She was walking very quickly
It was hard to make much ground
The crowds impeded progress
There were people all around.
Then I caught her at a corner
Where the crossing had a light
When I touched her on the shoulder
She was paralysed with fright.
And she didn't look delighted
When I handed her the case
Then a look of resignation
Slowly crept across her face.

It was when I heard her phone ring
As I walked across the street
That the blast within the brief case
Must have blown me thirty feet.
I've been stuck in bed for ages
As my life has been on "pause"
Why did such a thing of beauty
Choose to die for such a cause?

The Goal

A poem's just a load of words
It's letters; it's not real
It's funny how a good one though
Can alter how you feel
Some people think they're pointless
It's not a thing they choose
But sit and watch the football
Crying buckets if "they" lose
Yer pays yer money, takes yer choice
I don't care much for teams
I'd rather drift amongst the stars
In some words that fill my dreams

The Good Samaritan

I met her at a station
Or it could have been a train
The girl who came to help me
That I'll never meet again.
She picked me up and hugged me
Just to demonstrate she cared
And she showed some human kindness
Whilst the others stood and stared
I was on my way to rehab
I was lost and all confused
I was scraping long rock bottom
In a life that's lost to booze.
She sorted out my problems
Gave me hope to carry on
Then she helped me on my journey
And like an angel, she was gone
I don't know what her name was
It's a title of a song
It went down with the cider
And I know I'll get it wrong
But perhaps one day I'll meet her
When my life is on the mend
The girl who stopped to help me
When I needed such a friend.

The Killer

He clutches me so tightly
This boy I've raised with care
His body near convulsing
As he sobs in such despair
I've raised him from a baby
And I've done the best I can
From his first steps unsupported
To his big strides as a man.
His father left us years ago
When our son was not yet two
Then I tried to be both parents
But that's pretty hard to do.
A boy does need a father
A man to act as guide
To lead him through his early life
And be there by his side
And now my son's a killer
Though he says he weren't to blame
He always drove so reckless
And the end result's the same
I hear the siren coming
And we cuddle as we wait
His grip on me gets tighter
As the noise portends his fate.
The policeman rings the doorbell
He opens it...
I stare
His father looks much older but
I'd know him anywhere.

The Lidl Accident

I just caused an avalanche
In Lidl's Supermart
T'was when I pulled a cauliflower
It seemed to make it start
The carrots hit the onions
The turnips hit the swede
When at last it all stopped falling
It took two to get me freed
I tried my best to halt it
But I couldn't make it stop
Next time I choose a collie
Think I'll take it from the top.

The Little Boy

I don't know where he came from
And I'm not sure where he was
But I saw him on the news last night
And he touched my heart because
He was sat there in a corner
Head drooping in despair
As he clutched his little rucksack
Shaped like a teddy bear.
Don't look to me for answers
But someone help him please
That boy whose hope was drowning
In a sea of refugees.

The Long Wait

I'm standing on the platform
In the dark and pouring rain
In the faint hope I might see you
Let's hope it's not in vain.
I've heard you are returning
They said it was today
So I've stood here since this morning
As I have so much to say.
Been standing here ten hours
Met every single train
There's so much I must say to you
When at last we meet again.
My darling I am sorry
You did not betray my trust
It's one thing to be angry
But it's worse to be unjust.
There is a train approaching
Its shape begins to grow
The hope it brings you closer
Is more than you could know.
It's pulling in the station
Brakes halt it with a squeal
My heart is pounding in my chest
What will this train reveal?

The Magic Never Happens

His nose against the window
He surveyed the lovely toys
If only he could have one
Just like other girls and boys.
The train that went in circles
And the car that looked so real
He dreamed one day he'd get one
And wondered how he'd feel.
The window glittered brightly
It sparkled with its lights
His eyes alighted everywhere
On this wonderful of sights.
But magic things don't happen
Not even if you try
He'd watched the sky for Santa
But he'd always passed him by.
And slowly it got darker
As the store turned out the lights
He turned and left his dreams behind
And vanished in the night.

The Memento

Just found a thing that once was hers
A survivor from the past
A relic from a long lost love
That somehow didn't last.
Touching it, transports me
To a place that's far away
It's distance measured timewise
To a vanished summer day.
The fishing boats at Hastings
Neath the castle by the sea
Two lovers needing no one
Save the other's company.
I put it back and save it
In its long forgotten store
Replace it in its tiny box
At the bottom of the drawer.
I don't know why I save it
It's a thing she'll never need
But I'll wrap it in this poem
That I know she'll never read.

The Migrant

There is a child migrant
In an ever passing tide
Who dreams she'll have a Christmas
And she holds that dream inside.
Where she is, I know not
As she's only very small
In a sea of six foot strangers
She is barely seen at all.
I've heard she's lost her parents
And she's carried by the throng
She know's not where she's going
As she just gets swept along
The room is full of parcels
And she opens them with glee
Whilst she cuddles mum and daddy
By a stunning Christmas tree
I hope one day she makes it
To that Christmas of her dreams
Till then she's just a problem
Caused by politician's schemes.

The Naked Selfie

I tried a naked selfie
But the picture came out blurred
And the wife said standing naked
In December was absurd
Though everything erogenous
Had vanished in the cold
But any movement downstairs now
Is worth its weight in gold.

The New Day

This morning in the sunshine
The sky is clear and bright
The trees are turning vivid brown
Creating golden light
We all know what is coming
The winter's shadow's vast
It's nature's way of saying
Enjoy it while it lasts
It's time to put your boots on
Go walking in the leaves
It will lift your spirit higher
Than most things will achieve
This season is a blessing
There's the sun without the heat
As the summer's grip gets looser
It will soon admit defeat.

The Noisy Intrusion

The Robin sings a sad lament
Perhaps about last summer spent
Though long gone now, the summer heat
And autumn beats a slow retreat
The whole world lives without a sound
As nature slowly goes to ground
There's not much else that I can say
About this chill November day
Hang on though, I heard a sound
And there's not a lot of sound around
There it is, a distant roar
Where there was no sound before
Gradually the noise gets louder
And as a Brit I stand up prouder
There's no mistaking that great noise
It's the ghost of all our fighter boys
Suddenly the shape is born
A thousand feet above my lawn
Then it's gone, the sound declines
As do the hairs upon my spine
Why it came I know not why
But all I know, a Spit went by.

The Old Clock

The old clock in the hallway
Stands silent and forlorn
Yet it's run without adjustment
Since the day that I was born.
Been standing there two centuries
Seen people come and go
Its pendulum has marked their lives
By swinging to and fro
It's ticked its way through two world wars
Since the days of Waterloo
If only it could tell me
Of the former times it knew.
It must have seen adversity
Seen other times of joy
Survived attempts to open it
When its owner was a boy
But now it's fallen silent
And I swear the house feels cold
I feel a sense of tension
Like there's something been foretold
'Cos legend handed to me
Says the clock will cease to run
The day the earth starts drifting
Ever closer to the sun.

The Photo

It was underneath the floorboards
It was cracked and rather torn
A photo of a woman
Who was dead fore I was born.
She was captured in a moment
On a silver coated plate
Her beauty caught forever
Back in 1888.
The house she knew, still standing
It has outlived many lives
But of the world she lived in
Just her image now survives.
Her beauty slowly faded
As the passing years went by
I find her rather haunting
With those captivating eyes.
The picture I shall copy
Put it framed upon the wall
So everyone can see her
As they enter through the hall.
The photo, I shall place it
Where I found it as before
It belongs there with her spirit
In that void beneath the floor.

The Plumber

The plumber started sucking
All the air between his teeth
As he groped my boiler's testes
And the other parts beneath
Then getting up, he ooommed a bit
In a knowing way, to show
It was on the point of dying
And the bill was gonna grow.
"Your bladderstiddle's knackered
And your dooflang's on the piss
And I can't see how it's working
With an underthong like this."
I scratched my head in great surprise
And found it hard to speak
As the boiler was a new one
And he'd fitted it last week.
It wasn't bout the boiler
That I'd given him a call
It was just he'd left his spanner
By the table in the hall.

The Police Dog

Who said we don't have feelings?
Don't really understand?
I loved him more than you all did
We did everything he'd planned.
My world has gone to pieces
I've lost my dearest friend
You will all go home tonight
But I will never mend.

The Red Skin

I went to M&S today
I thought I'd buy string vest
One just like my father had
So I put it to the test
But I wore it in the garden
And the sunshine got me burnt
So with nipples now like hot cross buns
That's another lesson learnt.

The Reunion

"Scuse me, don't I know you?
I'm pretty sure we've met
I know your face from somewhere
But I cannot place you yet"

"I doubt it, I'm an Aussie
Though born here in this street
We left when I was four years old
So I doubt that we would meet
Though I had a sister, Lucy
Who died when I was three
We lived at number twenty
And she looked a lot like me."
I now know where I'd seen her
But I didn't tell her where
She'd find it quite upsetting
And that would be unfair.
I now live at twenty
And I know I'm not alone
The house gets very noisy
When I sit there on my own.
So the girl I've seen is Lucy
It must be her to blame
I think I'll try and call her
Now I know her name.
I bid her sister my goodbye
And head back to my door
The house now seems more friendly
Than it somehow did before.
"Lucy! Can you show yourself?

I've news for you to hear
Be nicer if I saw you
Then I'd know you're here."
Lucy doesn't show herself
But I feel her touch my glove
"Lucy, I just met your sister
And she sends you all her love."

The Shrove Chewsday Blues

Mother's pancakes were so tough
It's said they'd stop a bullet
And once when father's car broke down
We used one then, to pull it
They had the strangest texture
That was more akin to glue
Which made 'em really 'ard to cut
And even worse to chew
But no one said a single word
Just smiled and chomped away
Pancakes came but once a year
And how we'd dread the day.

The Sloe Gin Contest

"My darling, this is lovely
If there was a prize, you'd win it
Tell me, part from sloes and gin
What other things are in it?"

"My darling, glad you like it
I make it with such pride
And the only thing I put in yours
Is a dash of cyanide."

The "Soft Close" Seat

I stand and watch the toilet seat
Descending to the pan
I get the urge to push it
But resist it, if I can
Why does it drop so slowly?
As I haven't got all day
And I swear it will stop moving
If I turn and walk away.
I wonder why they make them?
It has never been a chore
To pee and shut the loo seat
Like I always did before.

The Spanner

It was merely just a spanner
Just a working tool, no more
But it wasn't what it was today
It was where it's been before.
My senses working overtime
Someone placed it in my hand
Only held it for a minute
It was more than I could stand
It conveyed a scene of terror
Much too scary to behold
A scene that overtook me
As it started to unfold.
The sea was taking over
In an engine room of steam
The bulkhead doors were closing
Such a nightmare of a dream
They said she was "unsinkable"
Greatest wonder of her day
When I handed back the spanner
There was nothing I could say.

The Stink

The town of Yubbadubba
Is a place near Abu Dhabi
It's nothing much to look at
'Fact it's old and rather grubby
It's famous for its camels
And its streets are lined with poo
And nothing smells as awful
As that Yubbadubba doo.

The Storm

The wind is howling like a hound
The surf blows cross the sand
No human voice can match this sound
Unless they're close at hand.
The waves in tumult hit the beach
Its pebbles thrown sky high
You feel unsafe till out of reach
You cannot help but cry
The sand is blasting in your face
There's nothing you can say
You hold her in a tight embrace
In case she's blown away.
Nature's in an angry state
She holds you captivated
Your ferry trip will have to wait
Until the storm's abated.

The Sunderland Bites

"U boat on surface, they're on the port quarter!"
"Do you think we can get there
Fore it's under the water?"
The lumbering beast
Alters course anyway
And the seconds tick by
In the hope they won't get away.
The engine note changes
Whilst they gather momentum
As they race in the effort
"To go and torment 'em".
"Hang on though Cap!
I don't think they've seen us
And the gap is now getting
A lot smaller between us."
"Front gunner! Bomb aimer!
Get ready for action!
I'll just get this ol'bus
To speed up a fraction."
The four Pratt and Whitneys start earning their keep
As the dive they are in
Goes from shallow to deep.
The engines complain and are starting to howl
And everyone hopes
They don't throw in the towel.
The wings all start creaking in the weight of the fall
And the pans in the galley start hitting the walls.
They are dropping so quickly
Like a coin in a well
And the old girl is screaming
That it's hurting like hell.
The men on the sub are starting to run

As the front gunner has them
In the sights of his gun.
They are safe at the moment
Till a thousand yards
A hit at this range
Is not on the cards.
The sub starts to sink
Down under the sea
In a desperate endeavour
For sanctuary.
But two big bore Brownings
Release hell with their power
And bits start to fly off
The submarine's tower.
Then "Bombs away Cap!"
And they now wait to see
If they'll make any contact
Down under the sea.
Time goes elastic, seconds are days
What the hell's going on
Just under those waves?
BOOM!!! They're all deafened
But no one shows glee
They've sent fifty men
To eternity.

The Suitor

We met in 1900
I found him rather cool
He said his name was Orville
He was handsome and quite tall
He said he'd built an aeroplane
And was planning on a flight
I knew that when I heard this
I'd found my Mister Wright.

The Swing

T'was a thing she'd always wanted
And she often asked he'd bring
But ol' Santa just ignored her
And he never brought her swing.
Then her days of toys were over
And she felt her wings unfurl
Her need of toys behind her
And the wants of little girls.
But I bought her one for Christmas
When she saw it, she went wild
At last the spell was broken
Of the disappointed child.

The View

I stand here at the window
And see the beauty roundabout
And compare it with the view I saw
From the room I started out.
No more dirt and chimney stacks
And smoke upon the breeze
Just my garden with its flowers
Plus the fields and lots of trees.
Don't feel the need for worldly goods
I have all the "stuff" I need
Don't mix with folk who want it all
With its avarice and greed.
Just this view is all I want
It's the place I love the best
I just pray the world don't spoil it all
Before I'm laid to rest.
I s'pose it's quite a humble view
It's not the Alps or Chamonix
But I can't believe I made it here
And that's enough for me.

Tinker

She's barely more than two feet tall
But when she plays, she's loud.
And has been known to scream so hard
She'd make a foghorn proud.
She has a little finger
So miniscule to view
But once you're wrapped around it
There's not much you can do.
Her secret is her bright blue eyes
That catch you in their gaze
A look that's so disarming
I'll remember all my days.
She's not a little angel
Up to mischief all the while
But I'll forgive her all of it
For one captivating smile.

Title

This poem is a short one
As I can't think what to write
You must manage expectations
'Cos the ending's now in sight
Too short to be a long one
It'll have to be curtailed
There's a full stop coming shortly
As a poem it has failed(.)

Toeing the Line

There is something fundamental
When you get the urge to write
An itch that must need scratching
That is very hard to fight.
It seems to grow in stature
Like a lion in a cage
Its form can be surprising
As it pours out on the page.
The ending comes to meet you
As the lines begin to grow
The best ones seem to happen
As they rise up from below.
From whence they come you know not
They just turn up on the screen
From the first line to the ending
There is little time between.
A moment spent in writing
Which you felt the need to do
Some poems are immortal
From a little bit of you.

Too Close to Home?

I walk along my boyhood street
And see it tho' through glass
On one side it's the present day
On the other it's the past.

First to see is Barry
He's standing at his door
It's great to see his face again
'Cos I thought him gone before.

Now there's Ronnie on his scooter
With his mop of ginger hair
After crashing in the street like that
You'd think he'd take more care.

Then I see the lovely face
Of a girl I knew from school
She smiles at me so sweetly
And she hasn't aged at all.

But it's sad to see old Victor
Standing by the track
He's waiting for a train to come
And he's never coming back.

More and more I meet old friends
But the image now's degrading
It's such a long time since we met
My memory of them's fading.
Now I peek through pub's front door
The place is full of laughter
Not a soul in there is still around

Perhaps I'll go there after.
I understand the vision now
It's a scene I've yet so see
All these people from my boyhood past
Are waiting there...
For me.

Too Hardy?

I tried to write like Tennyson
But it drove old Oscar Wilde
So I tried my hand at Kipling
But I sound just like a child
Then I thought I'd try Rossetti
But it came out more like Keats
So I just went back to Robbie
And accepted my defeats.

Too Perfect

She captures me completely
With her gestures and her waves
She acts just like magnet
I just can't avert my gaze
Her hair is soft and flowing
Her eyes a perfect green
She moves in such a lovely way
Most lovely I have seen
Her laughs are quite amazing
Her face lights up with glee
Can a person get more perfect
Than the one in front of me?
She's standing now, she's leaving
She's about to leave, it's plain
I follow her departure
As my daughter leaves the train.

Too Late

They found her in the bathroom
Lying crumpled on the floor
She had swallowed far too many
Then injected even more.
Her teddy laid beside her
Only witness to the scene
Her lifeless face looked older
Than her youthful seventeen.
Her Facebook ceased updating
And her tweets fell silent too
Her online friends were legion
But her real life friends were few.
Her death was in the paper
And got tweeted far and wide
Till each of her old school friends
Got the news that she had died.
The church was strangely crowded
Once the town had heard the news
They were standing in the doorway
Once they'd filled up all the pews.
She'd be shocked to see how many
Though with most they'd come to see
Few peers of hers were absent
It was just the place to be.
There were cards and lots of flowers
Lots of words to make amends
But she had no need of flowers
She had needed better friends.

Touching Thoughts

I remember how you touched my hand
That day we met by chance
I remember how you clutched my hand
One evening at a dance.
I remember how we both held hands
As we danced round in the rain
I remember how I kissed your hand
One day to ease the pain.
I remember how you squeezed my hand
As we walked back down the aisle
I remember how I held your hand
As you gave me my first child.
I remember how we clapped our hands
When she turned twenty-one
I remember how you gripped my hand
The day she had a son.
I remember all these moments
As my mind drifts through the past
I do it as you stroke my hand
On the day I breathe my last.

'Twas Back in 1980

That rotten car has let me down
In the midst of Markham Moor
So I'm walking back along the lane
That I drove along before.
The night up here is deathly black
And I rue my lack of coat
The fog's straight out of Conan Doyle
In a book I read, he wrote.
Hang on though, is that a car?
That's parked there on the grass
It wasn't there a while ago
When I had driven past.
It's ticking, so it must be warm
But the owner's not in sight
What I pray is happening
In the middle of this night?
As I'm cold, I try the door
It opens and I see
The light comes on and in the lock
I notice there's the key.
I blow the horn and flash the lights
Of the car that seems quite new
But no one seems to notice
So what am I to do?

I feel the need to take the car
And get the police to search
So I slip into the driver's seat
And I set off with a lurch.
Several miles later

There's a kiosk with a phone
So I ring up, just to tell my wife
I won't be coming home.
But she doesn't answer
Which is strange to say the least
So I drive on down to Markham
And I go to see the Police.
They view me with suspicion
And they check around the car
And in the left hand footwell
They do find an iron bar.
With a little further searching
There's a bloodied kitchen knife
And in the boot, the body
Of the girl who is my wife.

Two Letters

They're your Alpha and Omega
Your beginning and your end
The person you would die for
Attempting to defend.
Every life has one great love
They take with them to the dark
It could be in your childhood years
Or when you disembark.
Perhaps for you, a long lost love
Or someone close at hand
But if that love is yet to come
Please try and understand.
It is a truly wondrous thing
That beggars compromise
You all know who that person is
To see them... Close your eyes.

Uncle Edwin

The evening sunlight flickered
As I drove between the trees
Which had started gently swaying
In the cooling summer breeze.
I switched the car to silence
When I reached my journey's end
At the site of such a battle
I could never comprehend.
I walked amongst that silence
And surveyed the rural scene
Just fields of waving barley
Where the slaughter once had been.
Then in the far off distance
Heard a single tolling bell
From far across these very fields
Where uncle Edwin fell.
It was then I heard a skylark
That was singing up on high
As it serenaded sunset
In the cloudless Flanders sky.
A figure in the distance
Which appeared from out the haze
Was standing looking at me
As the colours turned to greys.
Then others seemed to join him
As the light began to fail
Their number grew to thousands
At this place called Passchendaele.
A century is nothing
In this valley full of tears
Those ghosts will be appearing
For another thousand years.

I strangely wasn't frightened
As I turned to walk away
Happy birthday, uncle Edwin
That was all I came to say.

Unforgettable

It was only just a single call
A simple thing to dial
He'd do his best to make it quick
Pay attention all the while
Glancing quickly at the keypad
He entered and pressed send
That's when he made connection
With the toddler on the bend
Many years have come and gone
But he can't forget the scene
He wakes up in the dead of night
As the small head hits the screen.

Utopia

We thought we'd build Utopia
In this green and pleasant land
The folk we blamed for all our woes
Were driven out and banned.
First we blamed the gypsies
Then we blamed the Jews
Then we picked on other folk
It was left to us to choose.
Things were getting better
Our world was on the mend
We didn't seem to care a lot
Quite where this all might end.
We shared out all the riches
Of the people we'd deported
And those who tried to stop us now
Were the next folk that we sorted.
The land was free of vermin
As far as you could see
It ended when the doorbell rang
On the day they came for me.

Waiting for God

I arrive and greet her cheerfully
And get the usual stare
There is no mind behind her eyes
For years, it's been elsewhere.
I sit and tell her all my news
But it's always just in vain
She wouldn't notice if I said
The same old news again.
She's waiting for her maker
But he never seems to call
Whilst younger and much fitter folk
Around about her fall.
She wants to meet her husband
Who died ten years before
She's no one left to dance with
And she wants to leave the floor.
All I get are vacant looks
A waste of time, it seems
She's somewhere drifting through the stars
In a head that's full of dreams.
The others in the beds around
Have mostly lost the plot
No one knows what day it is
And those that did, forgot.
The only thing she says to me
"It's time you said goodbye"
So I kiss her head and take my leave
And go before I cry.

Waiting for the 38

I'm standing at the bus stop
And there's a girl here on my right
She has the most exquisite form
Can't keep her out of sight.
Her hair's the hue of autumn leaves
Her eyes, a shade of green
Quite the most enchanting eyes
That I have ever seen.
Her nose is slightly pointed
With a gorgeous smile beneath
I love it when she laughs at things
'Cos she has such perfect teeth.
Her nails are all immaculate
And painted shiny red
And she waves her hands so beautifully
To endorse the things she's said.
Her top is thin and silky
And is tapered to her waist
It may not be expensive
But it shows she has good taste.
I sometimes catch a word or two
And her voice is soft and smooth
She nods her head at things she hears
Swinging earrings as she moves.

Damn it! Now my bus has come
I was hoping it was late
It's not often that I fall in love
At this stop by half past eight.

"Wot Really Dad?"

"There is a deer called Rudolph
Who pulls old Santa's sleigh
And he has got a nose so bright
It's used to light the way.
And Santa has a workshop
He's helped by lots of elves
And every year by winter time
There're toys on all the shelves.
Then flying round the world they go
On the night of Christmas Eve..."
How Dad convinced me this was true
I really can't believe.

Words

Just suppose, a juxtapose
Is a thing that meant the same
Instead of quite the opposite
Which is really quite a shame
The differences are tiny
'Tween a cognate and generic
It's much the same as airy
Which is not like atmospheric
Not sure why I started this
I'm afeared I'm on the tern
Which is something like a skua
But it's not a thing you turn...

You

You talk of your Ferrari
And your hols in St Tropez
You think that life's for taking
And you do it every day.
Your clothes are all designer
All "Armani His and Hers"
Your wife's adorned with diamonds
And a coat that's trimmed with furs.
She's taken by her driver
Who collects her from the door
To a restaurant in Knightsbridge
In a gleaming four by four.
You cannot see the food banks
Through the dark and soundproofed glass
As the Bentley whisks you homeward
Splashing puddles as you pass.
To you it's making money
It's the thing you love the most
But tonight my friend at midnight
You'll meet Jacob Marley's ghost.

Your Eyes

We haven't met for ages
Since I can't remember when
But I've thought about you sometimes
In a moment now and then
We departed much too quickly
Saying words that weren't too nice
Then those words became the issue
And we both then paid the price
But my cosy world got shattered
When you walked inside that shop
For me the world stopped turning
That's an awful lot to stop
I spotted you quite quickly
It was you, so plain to see
And then all around just vanished
There was only you and me
It was then you saw me staring
And I saw it in your eyes
It was more than I could hope for
And it took me by surprise
Your eyes conveyed such feeling
T'was the look that said it all
And it changed my life forever
Till the last thing I recall
I stammered just "How are you?"
And you murmured just "OK"
Then a man behind was calling
And you turned and walked away
You never said you loved me
But I saw it in that look
It was only there a moment
But a moment's all it took.

Zenith Over

The poetry had left him
He just didn't feel the same
He somehow felt more peaceful
And it went the way it came.
He was gazing at the ocean
With his mind upon the seas
When he felt his muse departing
As if carried on the breeze.
He almost saw it vanish
A suggestion in the eye
The spring that bore the poems
Had suddenly gone dry.
He stood there on the clifftop
Like a man who'd broke a curse
Tonight he'd sleep untroubled
By the need to write a verse.

That's all folks. I would just like to say a big thank you to two Bernies: Bernie Morris who got me started on poetry and helped me publish this little lot. And Bernie Rochester who drew the cover picture. Oh and thanks to Mandy Rigby, who sat and read it all, just in case.

Robbie.

The Ipswich Bus

Lightning Source UK Ltd.
Milton Keynes UK
UKOW02f0659270516

275089UK00001B/34/P